THE WOLF
IS COMING!

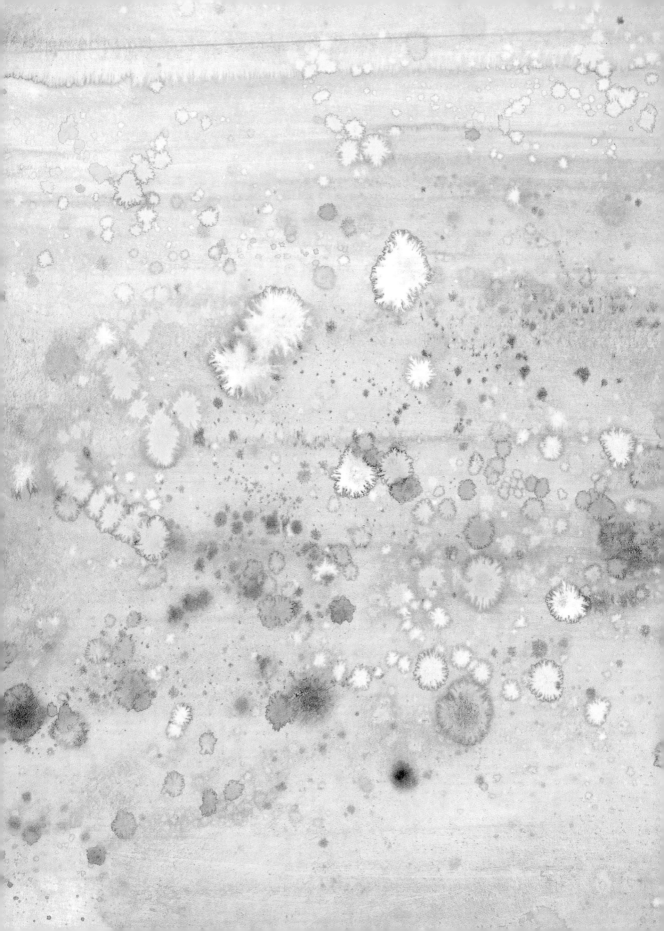

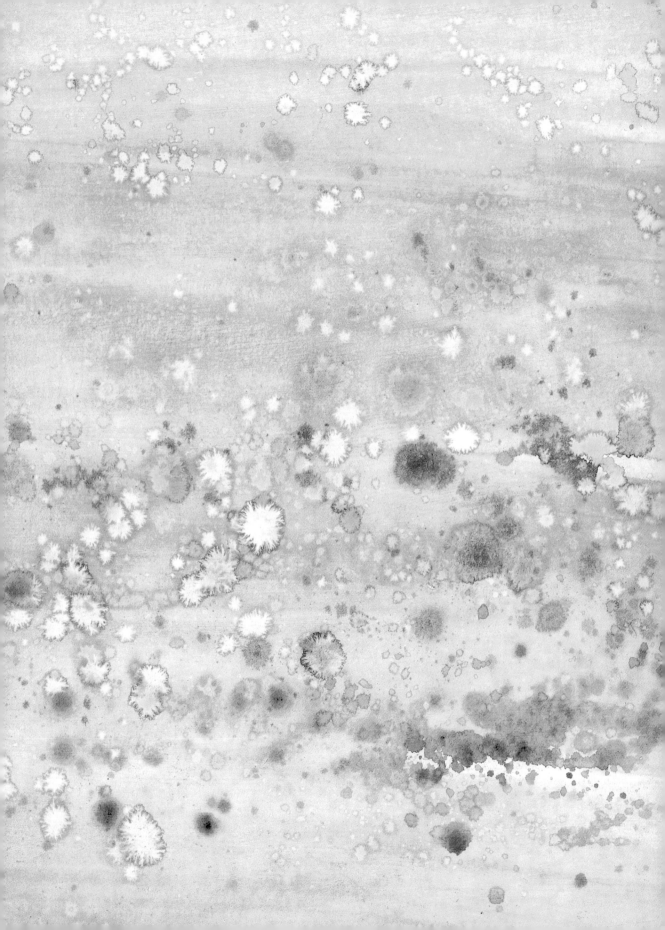

for Sylvia and Fraser – K.B.

First published in Great Britain by Andersen Press Ltd in 1997
First published in Picture Lions in 1999

1 3 5 7 9 10 8 6 4 2

ISBN: 0 00 664657 3

Picture Lions is an imprint of the Children's Division, part of HarperCollins Publishers Ltd,
77-85 Fulham Palace Road, Hammersmith, London W6 8JB.

Printed in Hong Kong.

THE WOLF IS COMING!

Elizabeth MacDonald
Ken Brown

PictureLions
An Imprint of HarperCollinsPublishers

A family of rabbits was searching for dandelion leaves on the hillside when a wolf came down from the trees towards them.

"Better start running, a wolf is coming!" cried the father rabbit, thumping his foot on the ground to warn the others.

So the whole rabbit family ran down the hill and through the fields, on and on until they were quite out of breath. And when they could run no more, they came to an orchard behind a farmhouse, where a hen and her chicks lived in a little wooden coop.

"Dear Hen, kind Hen, may we hide in your home?" asked the father rabbit. "There's a wolf about, and he'll catch us, no doubt – if we don't look out!"

"Come in, and welcome," clucked the hen, and they all squeezed into the little wooden house together. But just as the rabbits were getting their breath back, the hen peeped out of her little house and saw the wolf coming into the orchard.

"Cluck-cluck-cluck!" she cried. "We'd better start running, the wolf is coming!"

So the hen, the chicks and the whole rabbit family ran out of the orchard and through the farmyard, until they were quite out of breath. And when they could run no more, they came to the pigsty where a mother pig and her piglets lived.

"Dear Pig, kind Pig, may we hide in your home?" clucked the hen. "There's a wolf about, and he'll catch us no doubt – if we don't look out!"

"Come in, and welcome," grunted the mother pig, and they all squeezed into the sty together. But just as they were beginning to feel safe, the mother pig looked out of her sty and saw the wolf coming.

"Oink-oink-oink!" she grunted. "We'd better start running, the wolf is coming!"

So the mother pig and her piglets, and the hen and her chicks, and the whole rabbit family, all ran out of the sty and past the barn, on and on until they were quite out of breath.

And when they could run no more, they came to the cowshed, where a brown cow was looking after her two little calves.

"Dear Cow, kind Cow, may we hide in your home?" grunted the mother pig. "There's a wolf about, and he'll catch us, no doubt – if we don't look out!"

"Come in, and welcome," mooed the brown cow, and they all squeezed into the cowshed together.

But before they had time to make themselves comfortable, the brown cow looked out of the cowshed and saw the wolf coming.

"Moo-oo! Moo-oo!" she cried. "We'd better start running, the wolf is coming!"

So the brown cow and her calves, the mother pig and her piglets, the hen and her chicks, and the whole rabbit family, all ran out of the cowshed and down the lane, on and on until they were quite out of breath.

And when they could run no more, they came to the meadow
where the grey donkey lived – all alone in a rickety old shack.

    "Dear Donkey, kind Donkey, may we hide in your home?"
mooed the brown cow. "There's a wolf about, and he'll catch us,
no doubt – if we don't look out!"

"Oh well, if you must," said the donkey,
"but I'm not scared of a silly old wolf!"

All the animals scrambled to get through the door at the
same time, making a fearful din. There was thumping and
clucking and cheeping and grunting and squealing and
mooing until...

"QUIET!" brayed the donkey. "Everyone breathe in
or there won't be room for us all!"

At once the noise stopped as everyone held their
breath. But the donkey had only just managed to get the
door closed, when he saw the wolf only a little way away.

"The wolf is coming!" he brayed.

And, "The wolf is coming! The wolf is coming!"
shrieked all the other animals.

As they all let out their breath at once, the rickety old shack could hold them no longer. It burst apart, and there was such a commotion as all the animals exploded onto the ground that the poor old wolf was frightened out of his wits.

As fast as his legs could carry him, he ran back across the meadow, past the cowshed, through the farmyard and the orchard, on and on over hill and dale until he was quite out of breath. And when he could run no more, he came to the ends of the earth – and there he stayed.

So the cow and her calves went back to the cowshed, the mother pig and her piglets went back to their sty, the hen and her chicks went back to their little wooden coop – and the whole rabbit family went back to the hillside to search for dandelion leaves.

As for the donkey, he brayed as loud as ever he could until the farmer came to put his home back together again – and they all lived in peace for the rest of their lives.

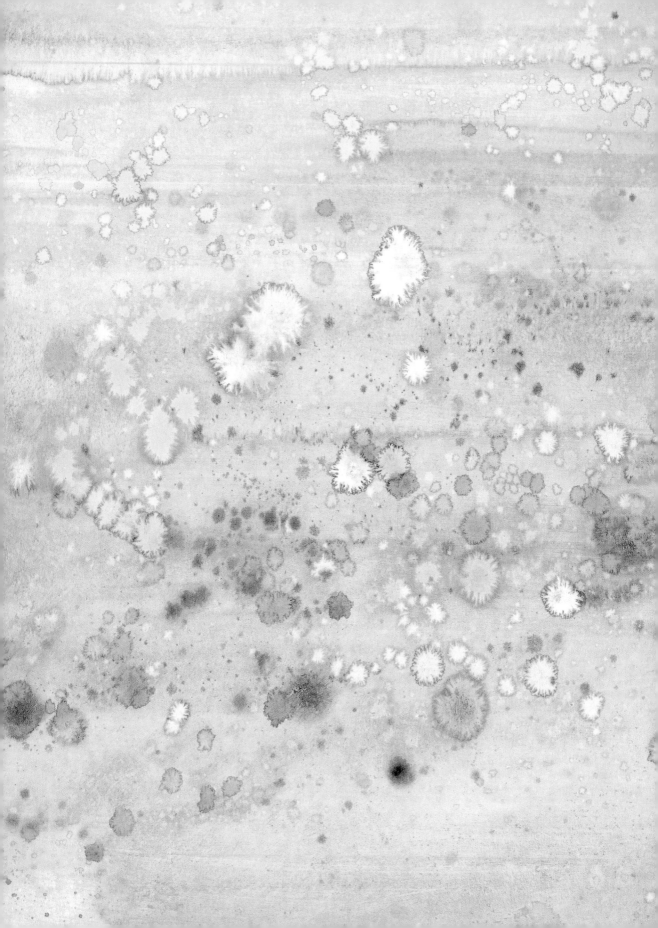

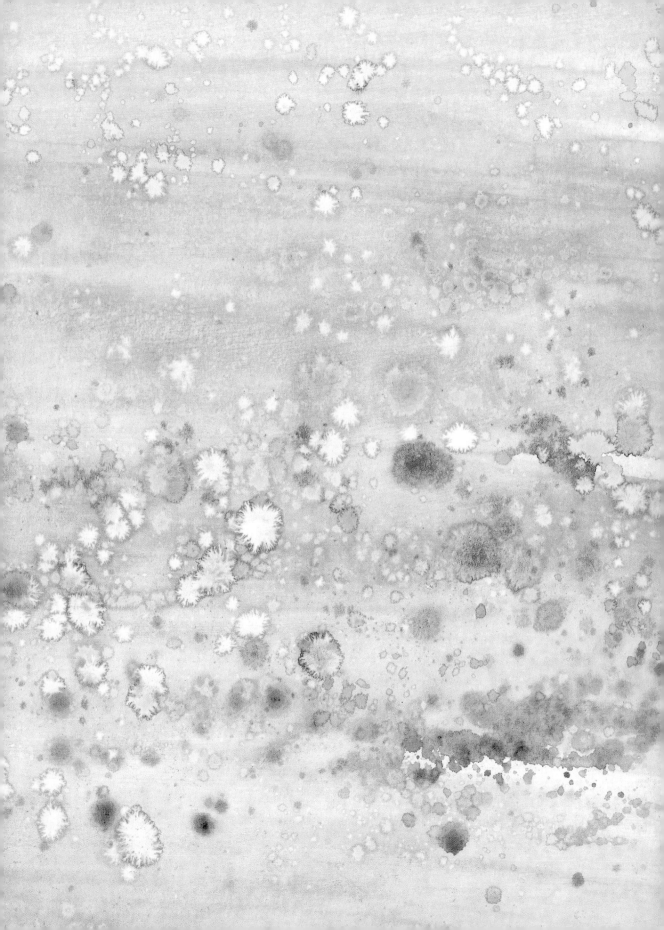